This book belongs to

....

Contents

5-MINUTE CHRISTMAS STORIES

make believe ideas

SANTA'S 12 DAYS OF CHRISTMAS

Clare Fennell • Alexandra Robinson

Have you ever wondered
what Santa likes to do
when his deliveries are done,
and Christmas Eve is through?

Welcome back!

He lands his sleigh on Christmas day, greeted by a cheer.

He's ready for a twelve-day break – it's been a busy year!

On DAY 1 of the holidays
he throws a yuletide ball,
with disco lights, red party hats,
and candy canes for all!

On **DAY 2**, Santa takes the **train**
through the **sparkling snow**.

He's off to see The Nutcracker –
his favorite Christmas show!

On **DAY 3**, jolly Mr. C

holds a **reindeer race.**

The **elves** stand by and **watch with glee**

to see who wins first place!

Finish

On DAY 4, Santa Claus decides
to skate with polar bears.

They swirl and swish around the ice . . .
and leap into the air!

13

On DAY 5, Santa takes his wife
to watch the town parade.
They cheer The Merry Marching Band
and praise The Dance Brigade!

On **DAY 6**, Santa's arctic friends invite him to the **park**, where, down the hill, they sled and slide

until the sky turns dark!

On New Year's Eve, the 7th DAY,

they all watch with delight

as fireworks

WHIZZ,

POP,

and BANG,

filling the sky with light!

On **DAY 8**, Santa takes some **yarn**
and **dazzling** glittery gems,
then **settles** in his **chair** to knit
warm sweaters for his **friends!**

On DAY 9, Santa and the elves enjoy the frosty weather.

They play snow games,

build tall snowmen,

Day 9

and take photos together!

On DAY 10, Santa plans to try
some recipes he's read:
three cream tarts, two fruit soufflés,
and a house of gingerbread!

On DAY 11, Santa Claus
prepares a roaring fire,
then sings some merry carols with
The Rockin' Robin Choir!

On **DAY** 12 of his festive break,
he **polishes** his **sleigh**.

He's **ready to start** making plans
for **next year's Christmas Day!**

The polar bear
who saved
Christmas

Fiona Boon • Clare Fennell

One Christmas Eve, in a den in the snow,

a polar bear slept and so didn't know

that her cub was awake. Pip could not rest –

Z
Z
Z

he was excited for Christmas,
the day he loved best!

POLAR
BEAR
HOME

In the **distance**, Pip heard a **jingling** sound.

He jumped up and **popped** his head above ground.

Pressed in the snow,

he saw **tracks** lead away.

He said to himself,

"It **must** be a **sleigh!**"

Pip walked through the snow

'til the jingling was gone.

Alone in the cold,

he soon missed his mom.

Fresh snow hid his paw prints

and covered the tracks.

With **no** path to follow,

would he **find** his way back?

But then the snow stopped,

and a blaze of bright light

led Pip to a strange and magical sight.

There were warm, cozy houses

and elves everywhere –

hope lifted the heart of the cold polar bear!

Pip peered through a window as he heard a loud wail:

"Dancer's broken her leg!

Who'll take Santa's mail?"

Inside was a sleigh filled with fine toys and treats.

Nearby, an elf shouted

and stamped his small feet.

The reindeer were worried –
they felt at a loss!
The elf looked around
and said (getting cross),

"We have seven reindeer,
but our sleigh needs eight.
If we wait for Dancer,
it will be too late!"

As they **pulled** out the sleigh, the elves made a fuss —
what could they do to save this **Christmas?**

An elf soon saw Pip and said,

"Don't be shy!

Can you pull the sleigh?"

But Pip said,

"I can't fly!"

The elves said, "Don't worry!" and put Pip in line.

"With your help,
we'll certainly
make it in time."

They **sprinkled** some sparkles and Pip gave a **sneeze!**

He felt **brave** and knew it was now **time** to leave.

Santa jumped on
and took hold of the reins.

The reindeer leapt forward,

so Pip did the same.

The earth fell away as the huge sleigh took flight –

and Pip and the reindeer
flew off into the **night**.

They leapt across rooftops, delivering toys
to the homes of all the young girls and boys.

In bed, sound asleep,

no child was aware

that Santa's new helper

was a small polar bear!

Pip and the reindeer worked hard through the night,
delivering joy on their magical flight.

The sleigh headed home when each gift was gone.
And though Pip was tired, they all cheered him on.

Then Pip saw his den – such a wonderful sight!

He slipped from the reins and took one final flight.

POLAR
BEAR
HOME

Cozy and warm

in the snow so deep,

curled up in his bed,

Pip fell straight asleep.

Early the next morning,

no tracks could be seen.

Pip looked around –

had it all been a dream?

But in the **snow** lay a **note**
and a **shiny** sleigh bell,

"For the bear who saved Christmas,
Santa wishes you well."

POLAR
BEAR
HOME

For the bear
who saved
Christmas,
Santa wishes
you well

The end

We Three Kings

Clare Fennell • Rosie Greening

Long ago, on a special night,
a star was shining clear and bright.
It glowed to show three kings the way
to see a baby, born that day.

King Henry, Fred, and Little Abe
had gifts to give the newborn babe:
some frankincense and myrrh to smell,
and blocks of gleaming gold, as well!

Before too long, they reached a land with **giant** dunes of golden sand.

"Let's all **roll** down!"

King Henry cried.

And so the kings began to slide!

Down the dunes, the three kings rolled 'til Henry said,

"I've lost my gold!"

He looked around, but searched in vain –
the golden hills all looked the same!

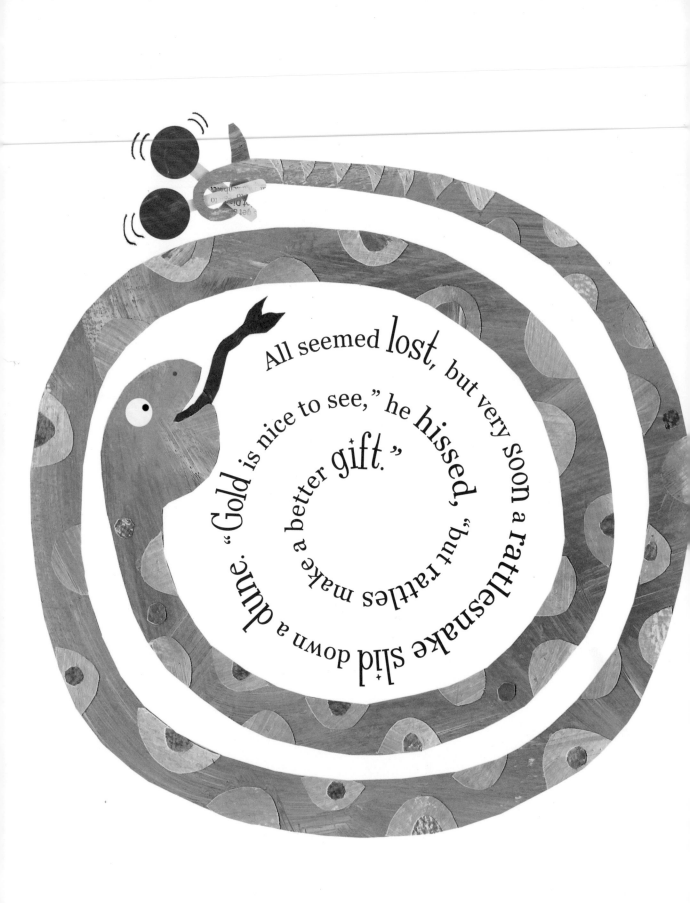

All seemed lost, but very soon a rattlesnake slid down a dune. "Gold is nice to see," he hissed, "but rattles make a better gift."

66

He gave his rattles to the kings.

King Henry said, "They're just the thing!

These rattles make a lovely noise –

the baby's sure to love these toys!"

The three kings held their presents tight
and headed off into the night.

"River ahead," King Henry said.

"I hate to swim!" exclaimed King Fred.

The river was both deep and wide,
with waves that
crashed
on either side.

There was no choice, they dove right in.

And then the kings began to swim.

69

Before the **three** knew where they were,

they heard Fred **cry**,

"I've dropped my myrrh!"

It sank down to the riverbed,

just out of reach for

poor King Fred.

71

Fred was just about to cry, but then a shoal of fish swam by.

"No need to cry! Forget your myrrh.

We've got a gift you might prefer . . ."

The fish brought **shells** for Fred to hold,
of **silver**, pink, and shining **gold**.

They hung them on some **silky** thread –
a **mobile** for the baby's **bed**!

Fred was thrilled and thanked the fish.

The gift fulfilled his every wish!

And so the kings went on their way

to where the newborn baby lay.

They walked for miles, by starlight led,

until a forest loomed ahead.

By then it was too dark to see

just where the forest path might be.

Poor little Abe tripped on a rock and dropped his frankincense in shock!

76

"I've lost my gift!"

King Abe **cried** out.

"It's **gone** for good, without a doubt!"

But just as Abe had lost all hope,
some spiders fell from silver rope.

"Frankincense smells nice," they said,
"but why not try our gift instead?"

The spiders used their rope to sew
a blanket made from head to toe
of flowers, buds, and leaves of green:
the sweetest gift the kings had seen!

Abe loved the gift, and so the kings

set off with all their brand-new things.

Then all at once the star shone bright

and bathed a stable in its light.

All three kings looked up and smiled.

This was where they'd find the child!

They crept inside, and there He lay

upon a manger full of hay.

The stable wasn't very bright,
with just one candle's glowing light.
The kings all bowed upon one knee
and whispered very quietly . . .

"We three kings come on this day
to bring you gifts from far away:

presents from the trees and sands,
from rivers and exotic lands."

As Henry, Fred, and Little Abe

laid down their presents by the babe,

the unique gifts shone through the gloom

and warmed each heart inside the room.

Soon the three went on their way,
but now each year on Christmas Day
we gladly celebrate and sing
about the gifts brought by the kings.

The end

Mr. Penguin's FIRST CHRISTMAS

Hayley Down • Clare Fennell

As the sun set on Christmas Eve,

a sound BOOMED across the South Pole.

CRASH!

Four little penguins walked along

and fell

into a giant

hole!

There, inside that snowy pit, was a funny-shaped, snowy mound

with two stripy legs sticking out and flippers that made a sound.

"What a weird bird," said Penguin Peg.

"That's no bird!" said Penguin Paul.

"Give it a poke!" said Mrs. Penguin.

Mr. Penguin said nothing at all.

Then something small burst out and cried,

"I'm no bird. I'm Ed the ELF!

I fell out of Santa's Christmas sleigh –

now I've crashed and hurt myself!"

Mr. Penguin felt bad for Ed,

but he was also a bit confused.

He asked:

"What's an elf? What's a sleigh? What's a Santa? What's a Christmas? And are you bruised?"

"Oh, bloomin' baubles!" shouted Ed.

"You've never heard of Christmas Day?

I'll teach you how to celebrate

'til Santa returns in his sleigh!"

"First, some sparkle is what we need
to bring some holiday glee."

"Let's try to find some twinkly treats
we can hang on a Christmas tree."

But in the snow, it's hard to find

decorations to gleam and shine,

333
333

96

so what the penguins used instead

were **fish**

and some boring,

old twine!

Ed said, "Next, we'll get kind gifts
to show our friends that we care."

"But remember, they should be thoughtful,
not just fancy, sparkly, or rare."

For Grandma!

The **gift** for Grandma Penguin was cute, but it wasn't quite **right**; it was much too **wet**, much, MUCH too **big**, and it gave her a little **fright!**

Next, the **penguins** tried a carol

and though Ed sang with a **smile,**

Mr. Penguin's horrid, screeching squawks could be heard for miles and miles!

"I've ruined Christmas!"

Mr. Penguin cried, feeling rather sad.

Ed said, "I don't know what you **mean** -

it's the **most fun** I've **ever had!**"

"This Christmas may not be fancy,
but the spirit we have is right.
Let's laugh and sing and just be glad
we're together this Christmas night!"

But then, Ed's golden pocket watch struck twelve with a jingly chime.

"Oh, no! The sleigh is almost here and I haven't made a sign!"

Mr. Penguin's family knew what to do; they had thought of the perfect gift!

They called all their penguin friends to make a sign in the snowdrift . . .

Santa flew over in his sleigh and from way up high, he could see some writing in the snow that said . . .

SANTA,
RESCUE

As Santa landed with a THUD,
he cried out, "Well, what a sight!
I'll spend the rest of Christmas here –
it's the perfect end to my night!"

They celebrated together,

then when it was time to say goodbye,

Ed promised that next Christmas . . .

he would be sure to drop by!

The end

Little Bear's
BIG ADVENTURE

Clare Fennell • Sarah Phillips

One fine winter morning
Little Bear awoke from a long sleep.

"It must be time to get up, " he said to himself.

"Look how bright
the light is!"

He put

on his

scarf,

picked up

his hat,

and

tiptoed

past

Mommy

Bear's

bed.

Little Bear opened the door
and was dazzled by the
shimmering scene.

The trees were wearing
white, fluffy coats
and the ground was as
cold as ice cream.

116

The Bear
Residence

DO NOT
DISTURB

"This must
be **snow**!"
thought Little Bear.

"How
strange
it looks!

I'm going
exploring!"

As Little Bear **set off** towards the trees,

he sang to himself:

"I'm walking through the forest,
I'm a very brave bear!
I'll climb a tree
and see what I see!
I'm not scared!"

From the top of the Big Pine,

Little Bear gazed at the snow-clad forest,

sparkling like

a million crystals

in the sunshine.

The forest

looked different.

It even smelled different!

Little Bear **jumped down** from the Big Pine. He landed on his bottom and began to **slide.**

He slipped down the slope, **faster** and **faster**, until **THUD,**

W h e e e

he hit a soft, white bank of snow.

"**Wow!**"he cried.

"That was amazing!

I'll do it again!"

And he climbed back up the slope, singing:

"I'm walking through the forest,
I'm a very brave bear!
Watch me go
on the slippery snow!
I'm not scared!"

Sliding was fun,

but after a while,

Little Bear began to feel lonely.

"I know," he said to himself.

"I'll make a Snow Bear friend."

So he got busy, pushing, piling, and

rolling the snow, singing as he worked:

"I'm walking through the forest, I'm a very brave bear!
I'll burrow and dig to build something big!
I'm not scared!"

"HELLO!" said Little Bear
in his biggest voice.

But Snow Bear did not reply.

"What's all that noise?"
said a sweet voice
from the trees,
and with a
"tweet, tweet, tweet,"
Red Bird appeared.

"What a great Snow Bear!" said Red Bird.

"But he needs some hair.

Wait here!"

Before Little Bear could say a word,

Red Bird flew off and returned

with a mouthful

of moss.

"Thank you,

Red Bird!"

said Little Bear.

"Snow Bear's

perfect now…

but all that work has

made me hot!"

"Try this,"

said Red Bird, handing

him a spiky icicle.

"It's a real tweet!"

Red Bird and

Little Bear

licked icicles

until they were

no longer thirsty.

"Thank you, Red Bird!"

said Little Bear.

"Would you like to come sliding with me?"

Taking Red Bird on his arm, Little Bear sat down and

whoosh!

Down the slope they went, slipping, sliding, skidding, and spinning

all the way
to the stream.

"WOW!"
shouted Little Bear.

"TWEET!"
cried Red Bird.

127

Little Bear stepped onto the ice
and found that he could skate!

"Look at this!"
he called to Red Bird
as he spun round and round
and sang at the
top of his voice:

"I'm walking through the forest,
I'm a very brave bear!
Watch me go
on the slippery snow!
I'm not scared!"

Little Bear skated along the stream and onto the pond, twirling round and round in circles until ...

THUMP,

he fell on his bottom.

OUCH!

Little Bear was upset.

He felt dizzy and cold and lost.

Two **big tears** rolled down Little Bear's face.

"Come on," said Red Bird.

"You're a **very brave** bear, remember?"

Little Bear looked at Red Bird. He couldn't manage a smile, but he did start to sing very quietly:

"I'm walking through the forest
and I'm a very brave bear!
To find the way back,
I'll follow my tracks!
I'm only a little scared!"

Slowly and carefully,
Little Bear walked back around the pond,

along the stream, up the hill, and past Snow Bear,

singing
as he went:

"I've walked through the forest,
I'm a very brave bear!
My home's in sight,
I can see the light!
I'm no longer scared!"

Mommy Bear was standing

at the door of the house.

"Where have you been, Little Bear?

It's not time for us to get up.

It's much too cold.

Come inside this minute."

"Yes, Mommy," said Little Bear.

"Bye-bye, Red Bird,

and thank you!"

"Tweet, tweet!" said Red Bird.

Mommy Bear gave Little Bear a hug and tucked him into bed.

"We need another long sleep," she said.

"When we wake up, the snow will have melted and it will be spring."

Little Bear felt tired and happy.

He closed his eyes

and Mommy Bear sang:

"You've been walking through the forest,
you're my brave Little Bear!
I'll say good night, then you'll sleep tight,
until the spring is here!"

And before Mommy Bear could say another word,

Little Bear was fast asleep.

The end

The Christmas SELFIE Contest

Clare Fennell • Rosie Greening

In a big, busy workshop
with shelves full of toys,
the elves worked their socks off
and made lots of noise!

They hammered
and clattered and chattered
and played,

and worked as a team on the toys that they made.

But Alfie was different from all of the rest.

He didn't like teamwork: he liked being best!

He'd boast about all of the toys he'd create,

then show them to everyone, shouting, "I'M GREAT!"

143

One morning, the elves

were so sick of his talk,

the Head Elf said:

"Alfie, please
go for a walk!"

So Alfie went out
to the gingerbread store,

and noticed a poster

he'd not seen before …

It said:

Best
Selfie

Santa is holding a

SELFIE CONTEST

so send in your photos and he'll pick the best.

Young Alfie was certain he'd win it with ease.

"I'll take the best selfie –
it sounds like a breeze."

He told all his friends,

but they just got annoyed:

"There's no time for selfies –

we need to make toys!"

SANTA'S WORKSHOP

Young Alfie ignored them and all of their fears.

He wanted to try out some selfie ideas.

He ran to the **polar bears** chilling outside.
"Please **pose** for a **selfie**!" he eagerly cried.

The bears made
a tower and Alfie yelled,
"CHEESE!"

But one of the polar bears just … had … to …
SNEEZE!

So Alfie rushed off to a whale in the sea.

He said, "Will you pose for a selfie with me?"

But as Alfie's camera went off with a flash,

the whale spurted water
on him with a SPLASH!

Then as it grew darker,

two owls fluttered past.

"Will you take a selfie with me?"
Alfie asked.

The group had a hoot, but it still wouldn't do...

the sky was too dark...

and the selfies were too!

Poor Alfie ran back
to the workshop in tears.
"I thought I would win,
but I'm out of ideas!"

"Forget about selfies," the other elves said.

"Let's finish these toys
with some teamwork instead!"

The elves got to work
and at last Alfie saw…

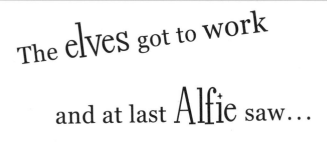

when they worked

as a team,

they could do

so much

more.

TOYS

WET PAINT

They **sanded** and **painted** with **painstaking** care,

and **soon** there were colorful toys **everywhere!**

"The workshop looks magical!"
young Alfie said.

And then an idea popped into his head ...

"Let's pose for a selfie!"

he said with a grin.

I LOVE
SANTA!

"With all of us in it, this selfie could win!"

He sent off the selfie and to his surprise,

he got a reply saying:

You've won First prize!

1st

I LOVE SANTA!

Your prize is a sleigh ride

with Santa himself.

Congrats on your selfie —

you're one lucky elf!

Young Alfie was thrilled,

and he knew what to do.

He showed all his friends

and said, "You should come too!"

When Santa arrived in his beautiful sleigh, the elves clambered in, then they went on their way.

And as Santa's reindeer soared into the skies, young Alfie was glad they had all shared his prize!

The end

'Twas the Night Before Christmas

Clement Clarke Moore • Clare Fennell

'Twas the **night** before Christmas,

when all through the house

not a **creature** was **stirring**,

not even a **mouse**.

The **stockings** were hung

by the chimney with **care**,

in hopes that St. Nicholas

soon would be there.

The children were nestled all **snug** in their beds,
while visions of **sugarplums**
danced in their heads.

And **Mama** in her 'kerchief, and I in my cap,
had just settled our brains for a **long winter's** nap.

When out on the lawn there arose such a clatter,
I sprang from the bed to see what was the matter.

Away to the window
I flew like a flash,
tore open
the shutters, and
threw up
the sash.

The moon, on the breast of the new-fallen snow,
gave the luster of mid-day to objects below.

When, what to my wondering
eyes should appear ...

… but a miniature sleigh and eight tiny reindeer,

with a little old driver, so lively and quick,

I knew in a moment it must be St. Nick.

More rapid than eagles his coursers they came,

and he whistled, and shouted,

and called them by name.

"Now, Dasher! Now, Dancer!
Now, Prancer and Vixen!

On, Comet! On, Cupid!
On, Donner and Blitzen!

To the top of the porch! To the top of the wall!

Now, dash away! Dash away! Dash away all!"

As dry leaves that before the wild hurricane fly,

when they meet with an obstacle, mount to the sky;

so up to the housetop the coursers they flew,

with the sleigh full of toys, and St. Nicholas, too.

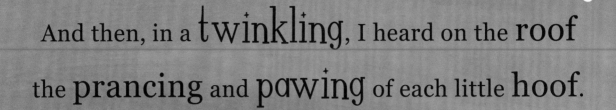

And then, in a twinkling, I heard on the roof
the prancing and pawing of each little hoof.

As I **drew** in my head, and was turning around,

down the chimney
St. Nicholas came with a **bound**.

He was dressed all in fur,
from his head to his foot,
and his clothes were all tarnished
with ashes and soot.

A bundle of toys
was flung on his back,
and he looked like a peddler
just opening his pack.

His eyes – how they twinkled!

His dimples – how merry!

His cheeks were like roses, his nose like a cherry!

His droll little mouth was drawn up like a bow,

and the beard on his chin was as white as the snow.

The stump of a pipe he held tight in his teeth,

and the smoke, it encircled his head like a wreath.

He had a **broad** face and a little round **belly**
that **shook** when he **laughed**,

like a bowlful of jelly!

He was **chubby** and **plump**, a right **jolly** old **elf**,
and I **laughed** when I saw him, in spite of myself.

A **wink** of his eye and a **twist** of his head

soon gave me to know I had **nothing** to dread.

He spoke **not** a word,

but went **straight** to his work,

and **filled** all the **stockings**;

then turned
with a **jerk**,

and laying his finger

aside of his nose,

and giving a nod,

up the
chimney
he rose!

He sprang to his sleigh, to his team gave a whistle, and away they all flew, like the down of a thistle.

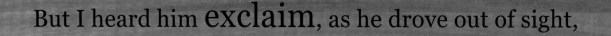

But I heard him exclaim, as he drove out of sight,

"Happy Christmas to all, and to all a good night!"

The end